We Need A Little Christmas

Leanne Banks

Description

WE NEED A LITTLE CHRISTMAS

By

Leanne Banks

When handsome cynic, Justin Dane Burgess rescues big-hearted Lilly Johansen in the snow, his life is turned upside down. Accustomed to avoiding intense relationships and the whole sticky Christmas season, he finds himself drawn into her life and learns to enjoy everything from drinking hot chocolate to decorating a Christmas tree and helping Lilly's elderly neighbors.

An orphan from a young age, Lilly has learned to create her own family wherever she is. Although Justin seems anti-Christmas, he sure is generous to her. She has been misled by men before. Can she trust her feelings for Justin?

Or will a bad choice Justin makes ruin their chance for forever love?

Dedication

This novella is dedicated to Linda Hogan and in honor of Cristy and Grandpa with special Christmas wishes to Linda.

About the Author

Leanne Banks is a NYT and USA Today best-selling author with over 65 books to her credit. She has won awards including two Romantic Times Career Achievement Awards and been a three-time finalist for Romance Writers of America RITA award.

www.leannebanks.com
www.facebook.com/leanne.banks

From the Author:

I was thrilled to write this Christmas novella for my wonderful readers. Christmas is one of my favorite times of the year, and the song "We Need A Little Christmas" brings back lovely memories of decorating the tree and singing along to Christmas music. If you would like to reach me, please friend me on Facebook at:

www.facebook.com/leanne.banks or visit me at www.leannebanks.com I would be honored for you to give a review of my story. I'm always happy to hear from readers.

Wishing you the best Christmas ever!
XO
Leanne Banks

Chapter 1

"Everyone wants something from me," Justin Dane Burgess muttered as he looked at all the requests on his desk. His retail company was busy enough this time of year without the requisite donation aspect of the holiday season.

His assistant, Francine Thomas said, "You don't have to contribute to all of them. You're very generous."

"You know it's Christmas. I don't make appearances, so I make donations to keep Frank Fashions and Home Goods in a good light to our customers." he asked.

"Or, because you're generous and have a good heart," Francine said.

"I'm not sure I agree with either of those." He signed several more checks.

"I must ask you about one charity," she said, clearly reluctant.

He looked at her with a doubtful expression. "Yes?"

Francine smiled. "That's all you needed to say."

"Ms. Thomas," he said. "I need more information."

"Many of the charities have requested your attendance at special functions," she began.

"Not interested in special functions," he said.

Francine nodded. "True, but I thought you might make an exception."

"Why?"

"Well, she just seems so nice and earnest. I don't think she's trying to win your heart. She just wants your presence at her event to increase its visibility."

"Hmm. So she got to you? It happens at least once a year," he said, signing another check.

"She gives coats to the homeless. She has given several off her own back," Francine said.

"Hmm. What great press for her charity," he said.

Francine sighed. "With all due respect, sir, you're too bitter for your own good sometimes."

Justin glared at his assistant, but she didn't waver or wither. It was one of the things he liked about his long-time assistant. "Are you saying I'm acting old, cranky and scrooge-like?"

"Stuck in your ways, sir," she said, pursing her lips and shaking her silver blonde head at him.

"I'm not a public person," he reminded her. "I hire people for that."

"Everyone needs to step outside their comfort zone every now and then," Francine said.

"And how have you done that?" he asked, turning the question on her because it was easier.

"I'm taking rap line-dancing classes," she said and lifted her chin. "What are you doing?"

We Need A Little Christmas

Justin blinked. The image of his senior silver-haired secretary participating in a rap line-dance nearly fried his brain.

"Well?" Francine said expectantly.

"I don't know what to say," he said.

"Of course you don't," she said. "Because you're stuck in a rut."

Justin wouldn't let just anyone speak to him in such a way, but Francine was one woman he trusted. "Leave the invite on my desk. I'll look at it tomorrow morning. I have another conference call tonight."

Francine frowned. "Are you sure you can't take a quick visit tonight with Ms. Johansen?"

"Absolutely not," Justin said and strode to his office. Francine meant well and she was extremely trustworthy, but Justin understood himself and humanity.

Everyone had always wanted something from him. Today was no different.

* * *

Lilly Johansen stepped inside the downtown office building and smiled at the security person. "I'm here to see Mr. Burgess."

The security woman rang someone else and nodded. "Fifth floor." She nodded toward a bank of elevators.

Leanne Banks

Excitement climbed with each passing floor. Lilly clenched her pink gloved hands together. The doors opened and she stepped into a lobby where a lovely, yet stern-looking silver-haired woman presided over a desk. Lilly knew this was Francine Thomas, the gate-keeper.

Lilly smiled again. "You must be Francine Thomas. Thank you for your responses to me."

Francine pursed her lips. "I'm sorry, but Mr. Burgess wasn't receptive to your invitation. He will give your charity a donation, but he's adamant about not making personal appearances. If you've noticed, you can't find any photos of him on the web. He's very private."

Lilly nodded. "May I wait here a little while just in case he changes his mind?"

Francine looked at her sympathetically. "You can, but I'm quite sure he won't meet with you."

Lilly sighed. "I'll give it a shot," she said and sank down on her chair, loosening her coat and removing her gloves. She leaned her head back against the rich wood-paneled wall and closed her eyes.

A vision flooded through her. *A long time ago, there was a young woman and a toddler on the street in the snow. The young woman had been her mother.*

Lilly remembered the sensation of bitter cold. She remembered how her mother, thin from disease, had hugged her tight.

4

We Need A Little Christmas

Lilly remembered her stomach growling with hunger as the snow swirled around them. "We'll be fine," her mother said. "You'll be fine." Her mother rubbed her shoulders. "We'll be warm and fed in no time."

How? Where? Lilly recalled, shivering, hoping.

Her mother pulled them into an alley and under the ledge of a building entrance. "Just rest," her mother said. "We'll be fine."

Lilly's eyes opened. Her stomach squeezed tight. She glanced around the office. Francine had left. The lights outside the office were dimmed. No sign of Mr. Burgess.

Sighing, Lilly rose and buttoned her coat and pulled on her gloves. Perhaps, she should make a list of donors to ask to attend the charity event with her. Mr. Burgess had been her first and only choice, so…

* * *

Justin finished his teleconference then checked his messages. Nothing that couldn't wait until tomorrow. He shrugged on his coat and noticed the guilt-inducing paper message from Francine. *Ms. Johansen was here. Wish you would reconsider.*

Justin crumpled the piece of paper and tossed it into the trash. He wouldn't be manipulated into attending a charity event just because.

As he rode down the elevator, however, he did feel a twinge of guilt. He hated himself for it, but it was there. He ordered his car delivered from the garage.

Taking a deep breath to move on, he stepped outside the building into the chilly night. Snow and sleet fell. The ice felt like needles. Midwest winters were unforgiving. He lifted the hood of his black cashmere wool coat knowing he had another just like it in his closet at home if he ruined this one.

The Jeep arrived at the curb and the driver handed him his key. "Have a good night, sir."

He glanced across the street and caught sight of a young blonde woman giving her coat to an elderly woman. He stood watching, unwillingly fascinated.

A second later, he saw the young woman remove her gloves and place them on the elderly woman's hands.

Justin forced himself to look away, but his determination didn't last. He glanced back. The older woman shuffled away.

The younger woman stared after her and hugged her arms around herself. Justin decided the young woman could call a car service. Uber was only a text away.

He turned away and got into his car, then gave into the urge to glance across the street one last time. Unable to see either woman, he searched the street from one end to the other.

We Need A Little Christmas

He finally spotted a woman down on the curb and felt a clench in his gut. He could call emergency or he could help.

Justin reluctantly made a U-turn to check on the younger woman. She wasn't moving. Stopping beside her, he got out and looked down. Her blonde hair was tousled against the snow beneath her. "You're not okay," he said, seeing that her eyes were closed, her cheeks and nose pink from the cold temperature. "Hello? Hello?"

Sighing, he picked her up and carefully put her in the backseat of his car. He couldn't leave her out in the elements waiting for an ambulance. But now what should he do with her?

Chapter 2

A nagging ache in her ankle awakened Lilly. Warm and cozy, she resisted the urge to fully awaken, but a male voice penetrated her conscious. "Are you awake? If you're not, I'm going to take you to the emergency room."

She recoiled at the idea of the emergency room. She was fine, wasn't she?

"One last try," he said.

"I'm awake," she managed and shook her head, lifting it at the same time. "What—" She glanced around the unfamiliar vehicle. It took a few seconds, but her brain clicked through her experience. She'd given the woman her coat and then she'd fallen on the ice.

She glanced up at the man in the front seat. Although he was handsome in a rough sort of way, he was totally unfamiliar to her. "Who are you?"

"I saw that you fell and thought I shouldn't leave you out in the cold on the ground."

"Okay, thank you," she said, trying to collect her thoughts quickly.

"Do you have a concussion? Are you in pain? Should I take you to the emergency room?"

"No. I'm fine," she said and she would have said the same even if she weren't fine. She had no interest in going to the ER. "I'm sure I can get a bus ride. Thank you for helping me, but you don't need to do anymore."

The man sighed. "Since you're alert, I don't mind taking you home. I just need your address."

"You're sure?" she asked. "You probably have a million other things you'd rather be doing."

He said something under his breath she couldn't quite hear.

"Pardon me?" she said.

"I want to take you home. I'll feel better knowing you are safe at home," he said.

She leaned back in the seat. "Well, that's very nice," she said and sat up against the seat. "I'm Lilly Johansen, and my street address is 301 Maple Lane. I have the second floor apartment, there. And your name again?" she asked him.

He hesitated a half-beat and glanced at her from the rear-view mirror. "Dane," he said.

"Well, Dane, thank you very much for rescuing me."

He muttered again and she couldn't make out his words. "Pardon?"

"You're welcome," he said, but he didn't sound all that happy about it.

Lilly half-dozed as Dane drove toward her home. He could have been an ax-murderer and perhaps she should have been worried, but she could tell he was a reluctant hero. Yet, a hero.

As he turned onto her street, she remembered she needed to check on her neighbors. "The

Tolinskis," she said. "We need to stop at the Tolinskis."

Dane pushed on the brakes. "The who?"

"The Tolinskis. They are my neighbors. I check on them every other night. This is the night."

He met her gaze in the mirror. "What is their address?" he asked in a not so happy voice.

She winced. "Not totally sure. I just stop by their house. Slow down. Wait. There it is," she said. "Would you mind terribly if I check in on them for just two moments?"

He narrowed his eyes then nodded. "I'll find a spot. Sit tight." He parallel-parked into a tight spot, which represented super skills to Lilly. Parallel parking wasn't one of her strengths.

As soon as he stopped, she pushed open the door and stepped onto the curb. She wobbled and winced from the pain from her left ankle.

"Whoa, whoa," he said, rushing to join her. "Are you sure you're not hurt?"

She nodded. "I'm okay, just getting my balance. I'll be better tomorrow. I have an ankle brace and boot."

"You've fallen before?" he asked.

"Tripped," she said. "I have a little problem with tripping."

He nodded. "Take my arm," he told her.

"I can walk on my own."

"Take my arm," he said in a firm voice and she followed his lead.

Her left ankle hurt a bit more than expected. "Well, darn," she whispered.

"What?" he said.

"Nothing. I'll be fine. A little ice."

"Are you sure you don't want to go to the emergency room?" he asked.

"Does anyone want to go to the emergency room?" she asked and chuckled.

He broke his frown and chuckled with her. "Probably not. However," he said.

"I've got a boot. I've got tape. If it doesn't work, I'll go, but now we need to check on the Tolinskis. Try not to scare them," she said.

"Scare them?" he echoed. "Me?"

"Yeah. You look a little scary with that scowl and beard. Try to look friendly. Think Mr. Rogers or Sesame Street."

Dane swallowed an oath. "Who are these people?" he asked.

"Children's programming. Think children's programming," she said and knocked on the door.

The door swung open and an elderly woman looked from Dane to Lilly. Alarm crossed her face. "Are you okay, Lilly? Who is this man?" Mrs. Tolinski asked.

"He rescued me after I fell," Lilly said. "I'm better now. I just wanted to check in on you and Mr. Tolinksi. Are you okay? Do you need anything?"

Mrs. Tolinski shot a skeptical glace at Dane. "If you're sure. We are fine. My husband is doing well. Using his walker today instead of his wheel chair."

"That's good news. Do you need groceries?" Lilly asked.

"We're okay for now. The church has brought us groceries and prepared food. But what about you? Do you have an injury again?"

Lilly flexed her foot. "Just a little sprain. I'll be better in no time. You know I'm prone to trip. A bit."

Mrs. Tolinski reached toward Lilly and gave her a hug. "If you need anything," she said.

"I'll call you," Lilly said. "I'm so glad Mr. T is having a good day."

Mrs. Tolinski nodded. "You take care and call me," she said, darting another suspicious look at Dane. "I'll check on you in a few moments."

"I'll be okay," Lilly said. "Good night now."

"She looked at me like she thought I was a criminal," Dane said.

"I'll admit she was suspicious. Maybe it was your beard," she said.

"What's wrong with my beard? I keep it trimmed," Dane said as he ushered Lilly into the front passenger seat this time.

"She's just fearful," Lilly said and shrugged.

"Why aren't you? Am I scary?" he asked.

"You picked me up when I was passed out on the icy pavement. You've attempted to deliver me home, but stopped at an elderly couple's house. If you had terrible intentions, I would already be dead."

Dane glanced at her. "I guess you're right. I'm looking for a parking spot near your address. Any other stops?"

"Not tonight, although I'm worried about my downstairs neighbors. I can take care of that tomorrow," she said.

"Another neighbor?" he asked.

"Yes," she said. Don't you check on your neighbors?" she asked.

"Not often," he said. "We're independent and private."

"But what if something happens to one of you?" she asked.

"The building has security and there's always 911," he said.

She frowned. "Here we are at my apartment. I can make it in on my own. Thank you so much for rescuing me."

She looked into his dark eyes and saw conflicting thoughts.

Sympathy rushed through her and she put her hand over his. "It's okay. You did a great thing tonight by rescuing me. You can go home and rest easy. Thank you," she said and impulsively lifted her mouth and kissed him on the cheek. "Good night."

Chapter 3

What the heck had just happened to him, Justin thought as he drove to his condominium. Except for sporadic intimacy, he had successfully avoided any sort of a relationship for several years.

His meeting, or whatever it was, with Lilly Johansen left him disturbed. In the short time he'd met her, she'd shown more humanity than he had in his little finger. Which made him feel like crap.

This was exactly the reason he didn't want to extend himself. He never knew what he could be getting into. Pulling into the valet for his condo, he tossed the guy his key. As he stepped out of his Jeep, he spotted something white in the backseat. He held up his hand to the valet and opened the back door.

Pulling out a fancy women's handkerchief, he thought of Lilly. This belonged to her. He would return it tomorrow.

The next morning, Justin rose and glanced out the window of his condo. Gray with sleet and snow. He wondered how Lilly was managing with her injured foot.

He probably shouldn't be thinking about her, but she'd left an impression on him. A Christmas angel, he thought, even though he didn't believe in Christmas or angels. He'd suffered too many losses during the holiday season to get excited about Jingle Bells.

Shutting off his thoughts about Lilly, he went to the office and attended to business. At the end of the day, he thought about calling Lilly then realized he didn't have her phone number.

He drove toward her apartment, rounding the street and sighting her at a Kindergarten/Day Care. She was wearing a boot and using crutches, so her fall must have hurt more that she'd revealed to him.

Justin drew into the traffic circle. A woman looked into his window. "Who are you here for?" she asked.

"Lilly Johansen. I think she needs a ride home."

The woman nodded. "Yes, she does. Call Lilly," she yelled.

Lilly hobbled toward the curb, essentials in a backpack, aided by her crutches. She looked toward him in surprise. "Dane?"

"Yes. It's me," he said, feeling a stab of guilt that he'd given her his middle name instead of his first name.

"You don't have to do this," she said.

"I want to," he said, feeling impatient. "Don't argue."

"Okay, okay," she said and maneuvered inside the passenger seat. "What a surprise. This was very kind of you."

"So, me being kind is a surprise," he teased, deadpan.

"No, I didn't mean to say that," she said. "This was just out of the way. Very impressed. I'm grateful."

"You forgot your handkerchief," he said, extending the embroidered cloth in her hand. "It looked like a nice one."

"Oh," she said, and bit her lip. "You have no idea what this means to me. I thought I'd lost it. This was my grandmother's handkerchief. I have so few memories from her. I never use this for sneezing," she said, laughing. "It's too precious for that."

He nodded, wishing he'd had some of the same memories. "Are you sure you don't need to go to the doctor?" he asked, looking at her brace.

"I've been through this several times," she said. "It's the same thing. I'll be better in no time."

As they arrived at her apartment, he stopped.

"Would you please come in for hot chocolate?" she asked.

He started to shake his head.

"I make the best hot chocolate in the world," she said, her wide blue eyes full of welcome.

"Does it include vodka?" he asked.

"No, but I can find something. Maybe brandy or red wine," she said. "Please come in."

Unable to refuse her, which was rare for him, he stepped from the Jeep and went around to her side of the vehicle and helped her to her apartment. She took the steps carefully one at a time and unlocked her door and opened it.

"Here we are," she said.

A very ugly, un-happy looking cat approached him.

"That's Mr. Happy," she said. "He only has 3 legs, but he's happy to be alive. Can't you see it on his face?" she asked.

Not really, he thought. The cat looked like the most miserable, cranky feline he'd ever seen in his life. "You were nice to take him in," he said, because he couldn't think of anything else to say.

"Relax on the sofa while I fix your hot chocolate," she said, still using her crutches to get through her apartment.

"I wouldn't feel right doing that when you're on crutches," he said and followed her into the galley kitchen.

She waved her hand in dismissal. "I'm young and strong. I can still manage crutches."

"It doesn't mean you should," he countered.

She shrugged. "Sometimes you just gotta power through. Have you ever had to do that?"

He thought back to his terrible falling out with his brother and nodded. "I guess so. But not physically," he said.

She giggled. "Sometimes I think I'm better on crutches than my feet. I'll be fine in a few days. Really. I've been through this several times." She paused. "I can be a little klutzy," she confessed in a whisper.

He looked at her with her blonde hair a bit frizzy and her eyes blue and wide, sparkling and felt something inside him shift. "Well, nobody's perfect," he muttered.

"Exactly," she said as she mixed the cocoa, sugar and milk. "I have wine and brandy. Choose your poison," she said.

"Brandy. It's cold tonight," he said.

"Sounds good," she said and dumped a generous portion into the hot chocolate. "Marshmallows?"

"No. This looks great the way it is," he said and accepted the hot mug from her. He jiggled the mug around a couple of times then took a careful sip. It burned his tongue, but warmed all the way down.

"Well?" she asked.

"I think you're right. You make the best hot chocolate ever," he said and took another slow sip. "Perfect amount of brandy. I thought you just sloshed it in, but you must have known."

"I sloshed," she confessed and when she smiled, a dimple appeared on her left cheek. "I'm glad you liked it," she said and took a small sip. "Do you like the Christmas season?"

"My business benefits from it, but I don't enjoy it," he said.

"Do you have family?" she asked.

Leanne Banks

"I do, but we're not close," he said, thinking of his brother and the betrayal Justin had experienced. "What about you?"

She shrugged. "My family of origin has passed away, so I make family wherever I am."

He frowned. "Family of origin?" he echoed.

"My mother and father died long ago. I was raised in a foster family. Now I make my family where I go. Like the Tolinskis."

He nodded slowly. He had the strange sense that Lilly's life was rich even though she had no real family and not much money. The notion made him uncomfortable. He took another sip of the hard hot chocolate.

"I give away coats," she confessed in a soft voice.

"Why?" he asked.

"Because people get cold," she said.

"Maybe they should just come in from the cold," he said. "Maybe they should go to a shelter."

"It's not always that easy," she said and took a sip from her mug. "Sometimes the shelters are full. Sometimes there are other issues. Have you ever been cold before?"

"Yes," he said. "Not for long, but I've been cold usually because I refused to wear a jacket out of rebellion." He paused and gave into his curiosity. "Do you have a particular plan? Or do you just collect some coats and give them away?"

We Need A Little Christmas

"Oh, I have a plan. Several local churches are collecting coats and the "Y" downtown has agreed to keep them to give away next Saturday. There's also a big charity gala. I was surprised to be invited to it, but I was and I wanted the CEO of Franks Fashions and Home Goods to attend, but he turned me down flat."

"Other than the obvious access to the CEO, why did you want him to go with you?"

"I was hoping he might be willing to run a special awareness day where people could get a small discount if they donated gently used coats. And Franks has locations throughout the state."

"Hmm," he said.

"You think I'm crazy?" she asked.

"Only a little," he muttered. "I know a few people in the retail business. Let me see if I can find someone to help you."

"Oh, that would be fabulous," she said. "I don't have dinner for you. Would you like to join me for pizza?" she asked.

Yes. No. "I didn't intend to stay this long. You don't need to provide dinner for me. I need to be going."

She nodded. "Well thank you again for rescuing me and my grandmother's handkerchief."

He nodded, taking another sip. "I'll let myself out," he said, and put his mug on the counter. He made it to the door and turned back to her. "Would you mind giving me your cell number?"

"Sure," she said and recited the number.

"Don't call for your pizza," he said.

"Why?" she asked.

"Just don't," he said and as soon as he left her apartment, he ordered a pizza for her. Half pepperoni. Half vegetarian.

Something about her bothered him and drew him to her at the same time. He needed to get her out of his mind.

Chapter 4

Lilly stared at the pizza Dane had ordered for her and her heart flipped over itself. She couldn't remember the last time someone had done such a sweet thing for her without even knowing her.

But maybe he had just been trying to get out of staying with her. He was quite attractive, yet quite distant. Probably not her kind of man.

At the same time, she couldn't help remembering how he had rescued her after she'd fallen. And then he'd put up with scrutiny from the Tolinskis. And then he'd returned the handkerchief. She looked down at the precious linen that dated back to her grandmother. The handkerchief brought her strength. Her grandmother had been strong. She liked to believe those qualities had been passed onto her. She hoped so, anyway.

Taking a plate of pizza slices with her to her coffee table, she propped up her foot and studied the spreadsheet for her coats for the homeless on her laptop. She wished Mr. Burgess would have joined her for the charity event, but his lack of participation wouldn't stop her.

Lilly liked to believe that every time she or someone else in her charity gave away a coat, that a life was being altered, if not saved. It may not be completely true, but she liked to believe it. And maybe Dane could help her.

A knock sounded at her door and Lilly rose carefully from the couch. Mr. Happy meowed at her as if he were fussing at her. Rightfully so, she supposed, given how many times he'd seen her in a boot and toting crutches.

"Coming," she called and looked through the peephole. Her downstairs neighbor, Roberta, a single parent and nurse working on her masters degree, waved back at her.

Lilly opened the door. "Come on in," she said and invited Roberta, her three-year old son and two-year old daughter inside. "Well, hello," Lilly said. "What a treat."

"I smell pizza," Marcus, the three-year old said.

"I'm happy to share," Lilly said. "If your mother's okay with it."

"You have to sit down and eat on a plate," Roberta told her son. "Lilly doesn't eat off the floor. Plus Mr. Happy might try to steal something from you."

Marcus immediately sat down on the floor. "I love pizza," he said, rubbing his tummy.

Lilly gave him a hug. He was a sweet chocolate kiss of a little boy, and his sister, Becca, was the most gorgeous baby she'd ever seen. Brown, with pink bows in her hair, Becca shyly smiled at her.

We Need A Little Christmas

While Lilly went to the kitchen to grab a plate and tray, Roberta sank down onto the sofa. Lilly placed a slice of pizza in front of Marcus. "Does Becca want a bite?" she asked Roberta.

Her friend shrugged. "We'll see. She's finicky." Roberta threw a sharp glance at Lilly's ankle. "What did you do to yourself this time?"

"Just a little trip on a curb. In the ice. Could have been worse," Lilly said.

"Uh-huh. And I could have sworn I saw a handsome man walking into our building. You want to explain that?"

Lilly bit her lip. "He rescued me after I gave away a coat and fell. He also returned my grandmother's handkerchief that I had left in his backseat. *And* he ordered this pizza for me."

"Oh, my. Prince Charming times three." She reached toward the pizza. "Looks like Becca is interested. Can I give her a bite? I'll try to keep it off the sofa."

Lilly waved her hand. "I've already had all I want."

"Good pizza," Marcus said, rubbing his tummy again.

"I didn't come up here expecting to be fed," Roberta said with a grin as Becca took a bite of pizza. "Thanks for feeding us. But you haven't told me enough about this mystery guy."

"I don't know all that much, but he's been very kind. At the same time, I've been invited to this big charity gala and Justin Burgess, the CEO of Franks, turned me down."

"Bummer," Roberta said and lifted a slice of pizza and took a bite. "Maybe you can ask Prince Charming to join you."

"I'm not sure he's up for that. He doesn't seem like the Christmassy type," Lilly told her.

"Hmmm. Well, there's a new doctor at the hospital who could use a little social life." Roberta took another bite of pizza. "He seems nice."

"Nice, but weird?" Lilly asked, a bit skeptical because Roberta had previously set her up with some socially inept men.

"He seems more nice than weird. I think you would like him. I know he would like you. Give him a go. He's lonely. Prince Charming may not work out. You need a date for this fancy occasion. He can step up. I'm sure he cleans up nicely."

Lilly hesitated then laughed. "Okay, okay. Thanks for helping me out."

Roberta took another big bite and shared another bite with her daughter. "Hey, my kids and I got fed. You have a date. This was easy. I just wanted to make sure you're okay. Marcus, take your plate to the trash, sweetheart. Don't spill anything."

Roberta watched her son like a hawk. "Good job," she said when he took his plate to the trash. She turned back to Lilly. "Well, thanks for feeding us. I'll give Henry your number. He's a nice guy.

We Need A Little Christmas

Call me if you need anything." She rose. "Come on Marcus. Tell Miss Lilly, thank you."

Marcus rushed toward her and hugged her. "Thank you, Miss Lilly. I love you."

Lilly's heart melted. "I love you, too," she said, hugging him in return.

"He's such a playboy," Roberta said. "Come on, now. Time for bed. Wave to Lilly, Becca."

Becca gave a sweet wave.

"Thanks for the visit," Lilly said.

"Thanks for being our neighbor," Roberta said and took her crew out of the door.

Although Lilly knew that Roberta struggled as a single mom and working at the hospital, she couldn't help longing for the sense of family Roberta had created for her and her children.

More than anything, Lilly wanted to belong.

* * *

The next day, Justin couldn't stop thinking about Lilly. Every time he saw a woman with long blond hair and a knitted hat, he took a second glance just in case it was Lilly. But of course, it never was. Irritated with his attraction to her, he reminded himself of everything bad that had happened during the Christmas seasons of the past.

His mother had died on Christmas Eve when he was ten. His father had died five years ago a few days before Christmas. And three years ago, the woman Justin had been somewhat seriously dating had eloped with his own brother again at Christmas-time.

December just wasn't his month. Although Justin wasn't particularly superstitious, he didn't want to venture into a relationship during this month full of losses for him. He decided to take action and approached his assistant.

"Ms. Thomas, I'd like you to send a notice to all our managers that we would like to donate 50% of our clearance coats for men, women and children. I'd like the merchandise pulled immediately and we will arrange for the coats to be taken to our local YMCA for distribution to those in need."

Francine stared at him shock. "Are you sure, sir?"

"Quite sure," he said.

"I don't know what to say. I'm just so thrilled and impressed. You must have gotten a chance to meet Lilly Johansen. Isn't she lovely? Will you be attending the event with her?"

"No. And she doesn't know who I am. When I met her, I gave her my middle name."

Francine frowned in confusion. "You lied to her."

Justin frowned in return. "I chose not to reveal my first name."

Francine made a sniffing sound. "Sounds like a lie to me."

We Need A Little Christmas

Justin agreed that he'd lied. "It won't matter in the long run. It's not as if we have a relationship."

"Well, that's a shame. A real shame because she's a lovely woman who wouldn't dream of taking advantage of you. I was so hoping you would see her charm. She could be very good for you," Francine said, all but wagging her finger at him.

Justin suddenly understood his assistant's ruse. "You were trying to make a love-match with me," he said. He should have been offended, but the possibility was so absurd that he couldn't keep from chuckling.

"Well, you could use a little help in that area," Francine lowered her voice. "You're a very intelligent man, but you don't seem to choose wisely when it comes to women."

Even though it was inappropriate for Francine to invest herself in his love life, he couldn't help appreciating the woman's sincere care for him and his happiness. "Ms. Thomas, I do appreciate your concern, but I must handle this area of my life myself."

Francine sighed. "I realize it's not my place," she said.

"That's right," Justin said.

"But this December could be different. This Christmas could be different. Remember that, sir," she said.

It was his turn to sigh. "I'll do that. So will you please get the memo ready for the store managers, so I can approve it and we can send it out."

"Right away sir. And if I may say, it's a fine, fine thing you're doing."

Seeing the faint sheen of pride in Francine's eyes made him feel uncomfortable. He'd spent a good part of his life avoiding anything overly emotional the last few years.

"Thank you," he muttered and returned to his office. Disliking the upheaval of strange feelings, he told himself that once he turned over the coats to Lilly's charity, he would be done. That action would give him a sense of finality and he could move past this unwelcome episode of emotion.

A message popped up on his cellphone from a woman he'd seen a few times. She was the antithesis of Lilly. A beautiful brunette, sophisticated, not too deep, but cheerful. She wanted to meet for drinks. A perfect distraction, he told himself.

Justin wrapped up his day just after five-thirty and headed to the cocktail bar down the street to meet Ava Gallimore.

"There you are Justin," she called and he spotted her waving at him and wearing a big smile. "Come on over. It's been way too long, handsome. The beard is great," she said touching his jaw and purring. "Makes you look rough around the edges."

We Need A Little Christmas

"Good to know," he said, feeling a little overwhelmed by the way she'd instantly touched him. But then he remembered that was Ava's way and part of her charm. "You're looking beautiful as usual," he said, noting not a hair was out of place and her cosmetics appeared to be perfectly applied.

She lifted her shoulders in a coy move. "Oh, you're just flattering me."

Not really, he thought, but wasn't going to argue the point. "What can I get you to drink?" he asked.

"I'll just have a teensy glass of wine. I must watch my calorie intake with the holiday season," she said.

"You don't look like you need to watch anything to me," he said.

"Oh, there you go flattering me again. Are you trying to get under my skin?" she asked with a seductive glance.

He waved his hand at the bartender who responded immediately. "I'll take an old-fashioned and the lady would like a glass of white wine."

"Savignon blanc, please," Ava said then turned to Justin. "Now, tell me everything you've been up to," she said.

"Nothing all that interesting. Just the usual, work," he said.

"Building your fortune," she said with a sassy smile. "Have you visited your ranch recently? I bet it's wonderful on the weekends."

"I haven't had a chance."

"Oh, well I'm sure I could help you relax," she said. "But I'm also sure a mogul's gotta do what a mogul's gotta do."

Justin had never referred to himself as a mogul. The server placed the drinks in front of him and he took a sip of his old-fashioned.

"I've been crazy busy, too. You wouldn't think the real estate business would be busy during the holiday season, but it seems like everyone wants to buy or sell," she said.

"Good for you," he said.

"Yes, it is. And of course, it seems like there are dozens of parties. I can hardly keep track of them. I'm sure you have the same problem. There's going to be a little get-together at the country club next week. Only about two hundred guests. Is there any chance you would join me? I would love to have you by my side. I know we take great photos."

Something clicked inside of Justin. This wasn't going to work with Ava. No way. No how. She was physically beautiful, but her personality grated on him like sandpaper.

He shook his head. "My schedule's already packed. I don't think I can make it." He gulped down the rest of his drink and motioned for the bartender. "Check please." He turned to Ava. "I've got to go," he said and tried to think of a way to soften his departure. "You look as beautiful as ever. Turning heads wherever you go. Take care, now."

We Need A Little Christmas

"Merry Christmas," she said. "Don't forget me."

This had been such a bad idea.

Two days passed and he thought he should check on Lilly. What if her foot wasn't better? It was a lame excuse, but he did it anyway. After work, he gave her a call. "Hey, this is J--Dane," he said stumbling over his lie. "I wanted to find out how your ankle is."

"Oh, thank you for calling. How sweet," she said. "My ankle is better. I'm just being super careful. I prop it up while I'm at home. I used the boot some during the day."

"Good to hear it." He cleared his throat. "Can I take you out to dinner?"

A long silence followed and he began to feel a little itchy.

"That would be lovely, but I already have plans. I'm taking the Tolinskis to a tree-lighting in the neighborhood. Would you like to join us?"

Oh, for Pete's sake. A tree-lighting ceremony? Stick a pencil in his eye.

Chapter 5

"I'm so glad you came," Lilly said as Dane pushed Mr. Tolinski's wheelchair down the street toward the park where the tree-lighting would take place. She didn't want to admit it to herself, but she was happy to see Dane again. Although he didn't seem to be a big Christmas fan, she was drawn to him. She thought he was kinder than he seemed to want to be, and it didn't hurt that he was extremely handsome.

"It was nice of you to join us," she said.

"My pleasure," he said. "It's a nice night for it. Not too chilly. No precipitation."

Lilly leaned toward him and took a whiff. He smelled good. She remembered it from the first time he'd rescued her and she took another whiff.

"Is something wrong?" he asked in a low voice.

Lilly felt her face heat with embarrassment. "I'm sorry. You smell so good. That's why I was sniffing you. Sorry," she whispered.

He met her gaze and chuckled. "I guess it's not a bad thing. Better than smelling like cow dung."

"Much better," she said, still feeling self-conscious. "Oh, look, we're just in time," she said as they arrived at the neighborhood park. "Are

Leanne Banks

you ready for the lights?" she asked Mr. and Mrs. Tolinski.

"I know it will be a beauty," Mr. Tolinski said. "It is every year."

Mrs. Tolinski fussed over her husband, arranging the blanket over his legs. "Are you sure you're warm enough? I can give you my coat."

"I'm fine," Mr. Tolinski said. "It's brisk, but I've got a cap on my head, so I'm set. You know what they say, you lose half your heat out of your head if you don't wear a hat."

"There's a new study," Dane began.

Lilly bumped her hip against Dane and shook her head. "We're glad you're warm, Mr. Tolinski. Let us know if you get chilly," she said and smiled.

It took a moment then Dane returned her smile and nodded. Her stomach took a dip at his expression. Something about him got under her skin. She couldn't imagine that he was truly interested in her as a woman, but she couldn't escape the fact that he had rescued her and checked on her and returned her grandmother's handkerchief. She probably needed to get over it, but she didn't know if she could.

The neighborhood community association director stood in front of the group of people and delivered a short speech. At his command, the tall tree lit with dozens of lights.

Mr. Tolinski clapped in approval. "It's beautiful," he said. "Just beautiful."

We Need A Little Christmas

"Yes, it is," Mrs. Tolinski said, taking his hand. "We have another Christmas. God has blessed us."

Lilly felt emotion well up inside her. She fought tears and swiped her cheeks with her gloved hand. Feeling Dane's gaze on her, she tried to hide her tears.

"You okay?" he asked, offering her a handkerchief.

"Yes," she said. "I just get a little emotional at this time of year."

"I understand that some people do," he said.

"My mother died near Christmas," she whispered.

He paused. "Mine did too," he said.

"Oh, no. I'm so sorry," she said.

He shrugged as if he didn't want to think about it, and in that moment, she learned more about Dane than she'd ever known before.

After the spectacular tree-lighting, the group looked at the tree for several moments. Lilly absorbed the moment. "It's so beautiful, isn't it?"

Dane moved toward her and put his arm around her. "It is," he said.

With his arm around her, Lilly felt so wonderfully warm. She could never forget how cold she'd felt all those years ago. Lilly snuggled against him and sighed.

* * *

Justin wheeled Mr. Tolinski back to the couple's apartment. Mrs. Tolinski couldn't praise him enough. "You are such a nice young man," she said. "I was a little concerned about you when I saw your beard, but you're quite nice. Lilly tells us your name is Dane. What is your last name?"

Dane blinked. "Grant," he managed, thinking of his mother's maiden's name.

Mrs. Tolinski nodded. "A good solid name. Thank you for taking us to the tree-lighting tonight. Enjoy your evening with our Lilly," she said then lowered her voice. "But don't enjoy too much."

Dane met the older woman's gaze and understood what she was saying. "Yes, ma'am. Have a nice evening yourself."

"We will," Mrs. Tolinski said and pushed her husband's wheelchair into their apartment.

"They are such a sweet couple," Lilly said.

"She's feisty," he said.

She looked at him laughed. "I guess so. Any chance you'll join me for hot chocolate?" she asked.

"Do you have any food?" he asked.

"Not much. I'm not a great cook," she confessed.

"No problem. Are you in the mood for Chinese?"

"That sounds great," she said.

We Need A Little Christmas

One hour later, they lounged on her couch, eating Chinese food as her angry 3-legged cat watched.

"I still don't understand how you ended up here in Springfield Park," he said, wiping his mouth.

"I could ask the same about you," she said, offering a bite of chicken to her angry cat.

"I needed a new start. I decided to take over a company and it turned out well," he said.

"Good for you," she said. "My start was a bit more humble. My mother died and I went into foster care. I attended college and graduated, but my foster mother died and my foster father's new wife wasn't all that interested in the foster children. So, I'm lucky because I have a way of making my own family."

Dane looked at her. "That must have been hard."

"It was," she admitted. "At the same time, my foster mother had taught me so much. She taught me how to love and make friends with people. That's why I love the Tolinskis and my downstairs neighbors. We all need each other."

"So why do you love Christmas so much?" Dane asked.

"It's the season of hope. We all need hope."

"But isn't it temporary hope?" he asked.

"Temporary hope is better than no hope at all. Any kind of hope goes a long way."

He shrugged. "I guess I just associate the holiday season with loss and bad relationships. A few years ago, my brother eloped with the woman I was dating."

Lilly's eyes widened. "That's terrible." Concern darkened her eyes. "Do you still have feelings for her?"

"Not really," he said and realized he hadn't for a long time. "But it didn't feel good at the time."

"Of course, it didn't. Well, we need to replace that bad memory with a better one," she said and pulled on her boots. "I almost forgot my tradition."

"What tradition?" he asked, confused.

"My tradition of lighting a sparkler the same night as the tree-lighting," she said and quickly limped to the kitchen and pulled a sparkler from a drawer along with matches. "You'll join me, won't you? Of course you will," she answered for him. "Everyone likes sparklers. Ready?" she asked looking up at him like an eager six-year old.

How could he resist her bright blue eyes and wide smile? Especially when he had no inclination to resist her. "I am. Where do we do this?"

"Just outside the house is a decorated tree. Let's go," she said, grabbing his hand and guiding him out the door.

"Slow down a little," he coached her. "You don't want to reinjure your ankle."

Lilly laughed. "You sound like Mrs. Tolinski. I'll be fine as long as I keep putting it up every now and then." She pulled out the matches. "You hold the sparklers," she told him and finally lit a match after three attempts.

Justin handed the lit sparkler to her and blew out the match. Lilly pressed her sparkler against his and both of them burned bright. The shared moment grabbed at him in a new way he couldn't remember experiencing before.

Justin looked down into Lilly's happy face. Darn if he wasn't starting to believe in some of this Christmas spirit.

After their sparklers burned out, they returned to Lilly's apartment and Lilly placed the sparklers in the sink to cool. Justin glanced at his watch. Although he was reluctant to leave, both he and Lilly needed to work in the morning. "I guess I should leave. Would you like to get together Saturday night?"

"I wish I could, but I'm going to the big charity event. My downstairs neighbor found a last-minute date for me. Someone she works with at the hospital. A new doctor in town. She's always trying to set me up. I usually turn her down, but this time…" Lilly shrugged. "Raincheck?"

Justin's gut twisted in a most uncomfortable way. "You bet," he managed, but he wasn't happy about it.

* * *

On Saturday night, Lilly put on the burgundy formal dress she'd purchased from a vintage clothing store. She decided to put her hair up in a twist. The whole time she wished she was getting ready to attend the gala with Dane. Even though she'd hoped Justin Burgess would attend the event with her to promote her charity, she now wished Dane had been escorting her. She would have enjoyed every moment with him. Instead, she felt nervous and uncomfortable.

Putting the finishing touches on her make-up, she heard a knock at the door. That would be Dr. Henry Carper, her date for the night. Lilly took a deep breath, grabbed her short coat and purse and opened the door to a young, tall red-haired man who visibly swallowed at the sight of her.

"Hi, I'm Henry Carper. You must be Lilly Johansen," he said.

She could tell he just might be even more nervous than she was. "Yes, I am." She extended her hand. "It's so kind of you to join me tonight. I'm hoping it won't be too much of an ordeal. I fear there will be speeches and awards."

"But maybe some good food, and I can get a sense of some of the people in the town," he said.

"What an excellent attitude," Lilly said. "Thank you for joining me."

We Need A Little Christmas

Although Henry was a friendly gentleman, Lilly couldn't help thinking about Dane. She could just imagine some of his humorous asides and observations. She wouldn't be surprised if Dane suggested cutting out early to go to a diner.

Instead, they lasted through the speeches and awards. "Henry, I believe I've had enough. Have you?"

"Yeah, I have a full day tomorrow. The food was great though. I'm a bachelor, so I'm always glad to get a good meal."

She laughed. "Well, I'm glad there was something good in it for you."

"It was really nice meeting you, too," he said as he escorted her from the hall. "I have a crazy schedule, but maybe we could get together sometime."

"I have to thank you again for bringing me." She didn't want to give false hope. "You've been a great sport."

Since the parking spots on her street were full, Lilly insisted that Henry drop her at her building. She wished him a good night and happy Christmas then made her way to her apartment. After exchanging her evening gown for pajamas, she poured herself a cup of hot chocolate and sank down onto the sofa. Mr. Happy sat beside her, clearly ready for some petting and attention.

Winding down, Lilly glanced at her phone and saw a message from Dane. He wanted to take her somewhere special tomorrow. Her reply flew from her heart to her fingers. *Yes.*

Chapter 6

Every day that passed made Justin more uncomfortable that he hadn't disclosed his true identity to Lilly. Although he didn't want to believe that she was all that different, he felt that she was. He decided to take her to his ranch in the country to break the news to her. Before he left, however, he told her the ranch belonged to a friend.

As he drove his Jeep into the driveway of his ranch, he felt a sense of peace and excitement.

"This is beautiful. You're so lucky that your friend has this place," she said.

"Yeah, I am. I get to visit as often as I want." He pulled alongside the house.

"It's fabulous. But we need to decorate that tree in the front yard," she said.

"The owner isn't here that often," he protested.

"But think how many people pass this house."

"If you say so," he said. "That means we need to go back to the closest store to get lights."

"Then that's what we should do. Now," she said, urging him.

"If you say so." He put the Jeep in reverse and headed into town. He and Lilly bought lights, lights and more lights then returned to the ranch. Mounting a ladder, she wound the lights from the top down to him below until the tree was fully encircled with lights.

"It's beautiful," she said when he turned on the lights. "Perfect."

Her smile made his heart turn over. He'd thought his heart was stale and unmovable. He opened his arms to her. "Come on down. You're making me nervous. I don't want you to hurt your ankle again."

She laughed and fell into his arms. Justin swung her around and inhaled her sweet scent and energy. "I thought of something else you and I could do today."

"What is that?" she asked.

"How do you feel about a horse-drawn sleigh ride? The neighbors will provide both," he said.

She gazed into his eyes. "Best day ever. And these are the best neighbors ever."

"I'll be sure to tell them. We just need to take a short walk to get on that sled. Let me make a call," he said and called his neighbor. Within moments, a horse and sled appeared.

Lilly clapped her hands together. "This is magic."

Justin felt as if Lilly provided the magic.

He helped her into the sled and they rode on the snow. She sang several snow songs, slightly off-key, but he adored her even more for that. When they arrived back to his ranch house, the sun was setting.

We Need A Little Christmas

"I wish this day would never end," she said.

"Me too," he said and lowered his head to kiss her. Her mouth was sweet, receptive and responsive. It was such a precious moment.

She finally drew back. "Thank you for a perfect day."

"My pleasure," he said. "It was perfect for me, too."

He drove them back to town, all the while searching for the best moment to tell her his true name, his true identity. But the moment never seemed to come.

Justin helped her to her apartment. "You okay?"

She beamed at him. "I can't remember having a better day. Thank you," she said and lifted upon tip-toe to brush her lips against his. Her kiss left him wanting so much more.

"We'll talk soon," he said, brushing his hands over her arms.

She nodded. "Yes. Thank you again." She turned and walked into her apartment.

Justin stared after her, wishing he had found that perfect moment to tell Lilly who he really was. He couldn't keep delaying. He needed to tell her.

* * *

Monday morning, Lilly nearly skipped into work. Her ankle was mostly healed and her heart was turning cartwheels over Dane. She believed she'd finally met a man she could trust with her heart.

Arriving early, she greeted her co-workers. "How was your weekend?" Sabrina asked with a sly grin. "Dating a millionaire must be nice."

"Millionaire?" Lilly echoed. "What do you mean?"

"This pic of the hunk who picked you up last week showed up on my newsfeed. Like I said, must be nice dating the CEO for Franks Fashion stores. He seems like a pretty nice guy. Gives all his full-time employees an extra day of pay or day-off after the holidays. You chose well."

"Where did you see this?" Lilly asked, thoroughly confused.

Sabrina scanned her phone and found a photo of a man that could have been Dane's twin. "Here he is. Handsome and rich."

Lilly frowned at the photo. "When was this taken?"

"Last week," Sabrina said. "I think one of the employees filmed him giving out awards. You don't look happy. Is something wrong?"

Lilly shook her head, trying to figure out what was going on. Why had Dane concealed his identity? "No," she fibbed. "How was your weekend?"

"Great," Sabrina said. "My boyfriend proposed to me."

We Need A Little Christmas

"Congratulations," Lilly said, glad for the focus to be taken off of her. "That's the best news ever!"

Later, after work, she received a call from *Dane*, but she wasn't sure how to respond, so she didn't. Lilly felt so confused and deceived. Why hadn't he given her his real name? Had he trusted her so little? Had she mattered so little to him? How could she explain his deception to the Tolinskis when she couldn't explain it to herself?

So hurt, she wanted to hide, Lilly refused to answer his calls. She deleted his messages without even listening. How could she trust anything he would say? She felt so foolish to have believed in him.

Four days later after she arrived home, she heard a knock on her door and felt a sense of dread in her stomach. She looked through the peephole and saw *Dane*, or who she'd believed was Dane.

"This isn't a good time," she said.

"Lilly, I need to talk to you," he said.

"I know who you are. You're not Dane," she said through the door. "You're not the man who rescued me."

"Yes, I am," he said. "Give me a chance to explain."

"Go away." She shook her head "Just go away."

"Lilly."

"Go away." She went to the den and put on her ear phones while Mr. Happy scowled at her. Mr. Happy didn't understand what it felt like to have a broken heart.

* * *

Justin immediately knew he had messed up, but he wasn't sure how to fix it. Lilly wouldn't respond to his calls and wouldn't even open her door to him. He didn't know what to do.

Justin worked twelve-hour days to avoid his failed relationship with Lilly. She was the one person who had sparked a light inside of him and now she had shut him down. He couldn't blame her, but damn, he had hoped this relationship could go further than a few weeks.

His assistant Francine confronted him on Tuesday afternoon. "Mr. Burgess, are you ill? Something is clearly wrong."

"It's the season. Christmas is our busy time. I want to support our locations as much as possible. I know the employees are working hard."

"Of course they are working hard. And you are too. But I fear something else is going on. Are you sure you're not ill?"

Justin sighed. "Lilly Johansen learned my identity before I told her."

"Oh, dear," Francine said.

We Need A Little Christmas

"She won't take my calls. Won't speak to me," he said.

Francine went silent. "Well, I suppose you don't need to worry that she's after your wealth."

He shot her a dark look.

"If she's worth it, keep trying," she said.

"She may complain that I'm a stalker," he retorted.

She shook her head and sighed. "You won't know unless you try."

Justin ordered flowers for Lilly, but received no response. He suspected she'd tossed them in the trash. He couldn't blame her. He called her a few more times and didn't know what else to do. He began to think that maybe he'd imagined their relationship was more than it really was.

He felt Francine studying him, but she was circumspect, for a change.

One afternoon, she approached him in his office. "Sir, your brother's wife has called."

"Great," he said.

"Your brother is ill."

Justin looked up at her. "What do you mean? Ill?"

"His wife didn't overly explain, but she did mention chemotherapy."

Justin felt a sinking sensation in his stomach. Was his brother Sam that sick? "Give me her number. I'll call back."

He gripped his phone so tightly he wondered if he would snap the device in half.

"Hello? Justin?" Marin asked. Marin was Justin's ex and his brother's wife. Justin pushed aside his reluctance to talk with her. He was over her, but not the way his brother and Marin had deceived him.

"Yeah, it's me. Justin. What's wrong with Sam?"

"He has cancer. The doctors are hopeful, but I'm so scared. I think a visit from you would really help him. He has lost his hair and the treatment is just brutal."

"Why didn't you call me before?" he demanded.

"You never responded before," she replied.

Justin's gut twisted in response. He just had not been able to stomach the betrayal from his brother and Marin. Sucking in a deep breath, he girded himself. "I'll be there tomorrow."

"Thank you," Marin said. "This will mean so much to him."

Justin immediately rearranged his schedule via his laptop and sent the update to Francine. It wasn't the best time of year to take away from the retail business, but his brother was more important. As he told himself that, he wondered if Lilly had changed his perspective. He wondered if his response would have been different before he'd met her.

Chapter 7

Lilly's cellphone rang and the number was unfamiliar. She let it ring an extra time then picked up. "Lilly Johansen."

"Hello, Lilly. This is Francine Thomas. Is this a bad time?"

Lilly was on an assigned break from her job with pre-schoolers. "I'm on a short break. How can I help you?" she asked, wondering why in the world Justin's assistant would be calling her.

"You may not be interested, but I thought you had somewhat of a personal relationship with Mr. Burgess. Although I don't really know. What I wanted to tell you is that Mr. Burgess learned that his brother is going through chemotherapy today and he is going to visit him. I didn't know if you would be interested in texting or calling him. Just a thought. I'm sorry if I'm intruding."

"No," Lilly said. "Not at all. Where does his brother live?"

"In White Mountain," Francine said. "But you don't have to go there. I don't even know how long Mr. Burgess will stay. I just thought he could use a call from you. Even as a friend. Thank you."

Francine disconnected and Lilly felt a well of emotion. What should she do? Should she call him? How could she not? Taking a deep breath, she mentally calibrated when she could call Justin later. At the moment, her pre-schoolers were waking up from their nap and wanted their snacks.

Later, after work, she called Justin or Dane, whoever he was.

He picked up after the third ring. "Hey. This is a surprise."

"How are you doing?" she asked.

"Could be better. My brother is sick. I'm here visiting him. He's been resting most of the time, so we haven't had time to talk. What about you?"

"I'm okay. How hard is it facing your sister-in-law?" she asked.

"Not that bad. It's been awhile. I don't feel the same about her. How's your ankle?"

Her heart twisted a bit at that question. "I'm doing well. Still elevating at night."

"Good," he said. "I'm glad to hear it."

"Why did you lie to me about who you are?"

She could hear his sigh through the line. "I can't explain this over the phone. I can just tell you I was wrong, and I would like you to forgive me. If you can give me a chance to explain, it still won't be perfect, but I'd like to try."

"Okay. Take care of yourself. We'll talk later," she said and hung up. Worry struck her. She had the sense that everyone counted on Dane… or Justin. But who supported him? Maybe that was part of the reason he hadn't revealed his true identity to her.

We Need A Little Christmas

* * *

Lilly took off the next day from work and drove to the community hospital in White Mountain. She had no idea how she would be received, but she just wanted to make an appearance for Dane. Or Justin.

After driving three hours, she walked through the sliding doors of the hospital and took the elevator to the fourth floor chemo level and strode to the waiting room. Justin sat there drumming his fingers.

"Hi," she said and he immediately looked up at her in disbelief.

He stood. "Lilly?"

Her heart skipped a beat. "It's me."

He raced toward her and pulled her in his arms. "I can't believe you're here."

She embraced him in return, but pulled back. 'I was concerned about you."

"Enough to drive all the way here?" he asked.

She nodded. "I'm not settled on everything. But I didn't want you to suffer this situation with your brother alone."

"Because you're my friend?" he asked.

"First. I'm your friend first and always."

His gaze full of turmoil, he turned toward a woman. "Marin, this is my friend, Lilly."

A startlingly beautiful woman extended her hand. "Lilly, it's so nice of you to come."

Lilly sat down in the waiting room and couldn't stay still for more than five moments. She had always hated hospitals. During her lifetime, nothing good had ever happened in a hospital. "Do you need food? Coffee? Anything?"

Marin and Justin shook their heads. "I don't need anything," Marin said.

Lilly paced the area. How could Justin remain still? She couldn't stand hospitals. How could anyone? Maybe it was inbred. Her memory was sketchy, but she did remember an IV, a warm blanket, and the murmurs of nurses caring for her.

"Poor thing. She's so sweet. I hope she finds a good home…"

"I'll get lunch for you," she told Marin and Justin. She just had to get out of this room. Too many memories were overtaking her. Even though she made it a habit to avoid hospitals, she hadn't realized how much they still bothered her.

Lilly escaped and found a fast food drive-through. She ordered several random items, including milkshakes and burgers and fries then returned to the hospital.

Marin stood. "I didn't realize I was hungry," she said. "Thank you."

"Neither did I," Justin said. "You brought enough for a half dozen people."

"I wasn't sure what you would want," she said.

He took her into his arms. "I'm just glad you're here."

We Need A Little Christmas

She closed her eyes for two seconds then pulled back. They had too much to settle. "Eat something."

"Thanks," he said.

Fifteen minutes later a nurse appeared. "Mr. Burgess has completed his tests and you may see him now."

"You should go," Lilly said. "I'll be outside."

"Won't you be cold?" Marin asked.

Lilly just smiled. "I've got a coat, cap and gloves. I'll be fine." Much better than she would be if she remained inside the hospital.

Justin walked into the examination room where his brother, Sam sat on the bed. Sam, thin and bald from chemo treatment, glanced up to Marin and gave her a weak smile. "The doctor told me we won't know the results for a few days, but he'll let us know as soon as he can. Thanks for coming, sweetheart," he said and she put her arms around him.

"As if I would be anywhere else," she said and Justin felt a burst of gratitude that Marin was sticking with him. Perhaps it really had been love between the two of them. Justin didn't have any feelings of longing for Marin.

Sam brushed his lips over Marin's cheek. "Let me have a few minutes with my brother. I know he's going to have to leave soon. Christmas is our busiest season, right, Justin?" Sam said more than asked.

"Okay," Marin said. 'I'll be right outside. Would you like a ride today?"

"I'll try to walk," Sam said.

Marin frowned. "Don't overdo."

"No need to fuss. See you in a few," he said and Marin left the room.

"What kind of ride are you talking about?" Justin asked, confused. "Isn't she going to drive you home?"

Sam chuckled. "Yeah. She's talking about me riding in a wheelchair to the car."

"Oh." Justin swallowed over the enormity of his brother's illness.

"I really appreciate you coming. It means a lot. I know it was wrong for Marin and me to sneak around behind your back."

Justin shook his head. "Water under the bridge. Don't worry about it."

"I know you sold your share of the business to me for less than it was worth just so you could get away from White Mountain." Sam pressed his lips together. "I hear you've done well since you left."

"I've done okay."

"Better than okay, but I won't argue the point. I just want to apologize for what I did and how I did it. I can't apologize for having Marin in my life. She's been great even after I got sick and lost my hair, energy and who knows what else."

We Need A Little Christmas

"I'm glad you have her. I just want you to get better," Justin said, gently patting his brother's shoulder.

"The doctor's hopeful. I'm working on it. I know you need to leave soon, but don't stay away so long." Sam slowly rose and took a breath. He held out his arms and Justin gave his brother a hug.

Strange, disquieting emotions ripped through. "Get well," Justin said. "I can hang around awhile this afternoon."

"Thanks."

Chapter 8

Justin waited until Marin left with his brother then he found Lilly walking along the edge of the parking lot. It was cold enough to see vapor when she exhaled. He wondered why she had insisted on staying outside when the temperatures were so frigid. He watched her for a moment and could easily imagine her stomping around in boots as a little girl. She still had the innocence of a little girl.

Walking toward her, he saw the moment she spotted him. She waited for him to come to her. That was something that had changed. Before she'd felt deceived she would have walked toward him with a glowing smile on her face. The loss pinched at him.

"How is he?" she asked.

"Weak. He keeps saying the doctors are optimistic. I hope they're right. We had time to talk for a few minutes. He apologized. I'm more than ready to let it go. I'll go see him a little longer this afternoon then head back. Can you come over to their house for awhile?"

"Just a little bit. I have to get back. It's my night to check on the Tolinskis. They count on me." She kicked at a melting piece of ice.

"A lot of people do," he said.

"A lot of people count on you, too," she returned, her expression reserved. "I'll follow you in my car."

Justin got into his Jeep and frowned in confusion. She'd driven this far to see him, but he could tell she didn't trust him. The way she looked at him made his gut knot. Lilly would be the best friend anyone could have, but it was tough for him because he'd seen her look at him with a sparkle in her eyes. The spark was gone. He wondered if he could get it back. He wondered if she would ever be able to trust him like she had before.

She followed him into his brother's circular driveway. His brother's home was a three-story Dutch Colonial decorated with only the best furniture. Justin knew, however, that the atmosphere in the house was tense and sad. He wondered how Lilly would respond to it.

Marin descended the staircase as Justin and Lilly entered the house. "Sam's already in bed. He gets exhausted so easily. He told me to wake him before you leave. A neighbor dropped off some soup. Would either of you like something to eat?"

"I'm not hungry," Justin said. "I inhaled that burger and fries Lilly brought to the hospital."

"I'm not hungry either," Lilly said. "You have a beautiful home. Is there something we can do for you while we're here?"

We Need A Little Christmas

"I think we're good. The cleaning service came last week. Same for the lawn service. I keep intending to put up the Christmas tree, but—"

Justin saw Lilly's eyes light up. "Let's do that. We can have that up in no time."

"I don't know," Marin said. "I have a ton of decorator ornaments and I have to be honest, I don't know if either Sam or I will feel like taking it down after Christmas."

"Then let's do a scaled-down version and use your largest ornaments," Lilly suggested. "Large ornaments take up a lot of space. Less ornaments make for less work. You'll be surprised what a difference having a lit tree will do for your mood. It will be good for both of you. Maybe we could put on a little Christmas music, but not too loud. We don't want to awaken Sam."

"If you say so. The tree and ornaments are in the attic," Marin said. "I'll heat up some apple cider."

For the next two hours, Justin supplied the muscle, Marin served apple cider and cookies and Lilly put the lights and ornaments on the tree in record time. She consulted Marin several times. "Will this do?"

Tears filled Marin's eyes. "I don't know what to say. I can't believe how quickly you did this."

"Me either," Justin muttered.

Lilly shrugged. "I have a thing about Christmas trees. Looking at them just makes me feel better."

"Exactly," Marin said.

Sam appeared in the doorway and smiled at the tree. "You had a party while I took a nap."

Marin walked toward him and hugged him. "Lilly and Justin put it up. She's fast."

"I'm Sam," Justin's brother said, stepping forward and extending his hand.

Lilly shook his hand and nodded. "Very nice to meet you and I enjoyed helping with your tree."

"Thank you." He glanced from her to his brother. "And how do you know Justin?"

"We're friends," she said simply. "I hate to trim and go, but I need to get back to check on my neighbors. I hope you'll be on the mend soon."

"Thank you again," he said. "I feel like a Christmas fairy popped in."

"Pretty close." Justin turned to Lilly. "I'll walk you out."

As soon as she arrived at her car, Lilly opened the door and turned to look at Justin. "That was fun. I think they'll enjoy it."

"That's putting it mildly. I really appreciate it. You worked hard," he said.

"Fun work," she said. "I hope the rest of your visit will go well."

We Need A Little Christmas

He wanted to take her in his arms, but she'd wrapped her own arms around herself and he could see she wasn't ready. "Be safe driving home."

"I will. You, too, Dane," she said then corrected herself. "Justin." And his deception hung like a curtain between them.

Lilly arrived back in town and situated her Volkswagon into a tight spot near the Tolinski's apartment. Although her ankle was sore, she carefully stood on a chair and changed a light for the couple. Mrs. Tolinski gave her a plate of cookies and cake as she left. Lilly planned on the sweets for dinner, but stopped by Roberta's apartment first.

Knocking on the door, she heard scrambling and Marcus yelling something at his mother. Roberta yelled something back at him and opened the door with Becca on her hip. "Well, hello there, Miss Lilly. I haven't seen you in a few days. Dr. Carper told me he enjoyed the evening with you. Why don't you come in and join us? Disney movie night, chicken tenders and popcorn."

"I can't imagine a better invitation," Lilly said. "I can contribute cake and cookies from Mrs. Tolinski."

"Well, that tops everything." She led the way into the den of her apartment.

"Hi, Miss Lilly," Marcus said, flashing his dimple at her.

"Hi, Mr. Marcus, are you looking forward to the movie?"

He clapped his hands with enthusiasm. "And the popcorn."

"They'll probably both fall asleep halfway through the movie. I've had them outside today to get rid of excess energy. Let me get some chicken tenders for you," Roberta said.

"No need. I can serve myself." Lilly got a plate from the cupboard. She had shared meals with the family before. "Oh, look. You even have sauces."

Roberta laughed. "You sound just like my little one."

"I'm hungry. I've been on the road today," Lilly said and stuffed a chicken tender in her mouth.

Roberta turned on the movie and set Becca on the floor. "Really. Where have you been?"

"White Mountain." Lilly shook her head. "It's a long story. I don't want you to miss the movie."

"Are you kidding? I've seen this movie three other times. I can quote it from beginning to end. Why in the world did you go to White Mountain?"

"Well, you may remember the man who rescued me a couple of weeks ago. His name was Dane Grant." Her stomach twisted. "Or, that's what he told me his name was."

"Oh, no," Roberta said. "Did you find another faker? Was he married with children? Let me at him."

"No. It wasn't that bad." Lilly took a breath. "Well, I guess it wasn't. I'm not sure. It turns out he is really Justin Burgess, CEO of Franks Fashions and Home Goods."

Roberta's eyes widened. "Oh, my gosh. You're joking. Well, why did he lie about who he was? That's totally sketchy."

"I know and I found out from someone at work. I was falling for him. It was just bad. I tried to write him off, but his assistant called to tell me Dane—Justin went to see his brother because his brother has cancer. But Justin," she said deliberately, "and his brother had a falling out several years ago, so I felt like I should show some support."

"By driving all the way to White Mountain and back in one day?" Roberta asked.

Lilly lifted her shoulder. "I would do that for you. I would do that for a friend."

"Hmmm." Roberta gave her a considering look. "You really think you can keep him as just a friend?"

"He's been generous to me and my charity, but I don't trust him."

"My mama always told me if you can't trust a man, then you need to toss him into the ocean like a bad fish. Don't spend your life living with a smelly fish."

Chapter 9

During the next two days, Lilly received several calls from Justin, but she neither answered nor returned them. She kept thinking about Roberta's bad fish analogy. The trouble with the stinky fish comparison was that she remembered how good Justin smelled. A clean masculine scent with just a hint of cologne, or maybe it was just his shampoo that smelled so good. Either way, she might not be responding to him, but he was on her mind.

She spent several evenings working at the "Y" in preparation for the coat distribution on Saturday. After arriving home to find Mr. Happy glaring at her in disapproval, she fixed a peanut butter sandwich and heated a can of soup for her gourmet dinner. She gave Mr. Happy a little extra cat food to appease him. He ate it quickly and sat beside her on the sofa, ready for her to pet and lavish him with affection. Lilly was too hungry to respond immediately, so he left the sofa in a huff.

A knock sounded at her door and she felt a sense of unease. It could be Roberta, but she usually put her kids to bed by 8 o'clock. It was now 8:30 pm. Lilly put her soup and sandwich on a tray on her sofa table and rose. Looking through the peephole, she spotted Justin and her heart leapt. She winced at the sensation and braced herself then opened the door. But not all the way.

"Hi. I wasn't expecting you." She tried to sound stern and unwelcoming.

He lifted a bag and shook it. "I have two subs, chicken soup and a chef salad."

Lilly barely resisted the urge to rip the bag from his hands. Her mouth was already watering. She could pack the peanut butter sandwich for lunch tomorrow and put the canned soup in the fridge. "Come on in," she said.

"I didn't mean to interrupt your dinner," he said as she packed up her yucky meal.

"No worries. I can eat this later. Have a seat. I'm sure Mr. Happy will be glad to see you." She put her leftover soup in the fridge.

"I doubt that," he said in a dry tone. Yet, the cat swirled around his legs.

"He's not very happy with me. I've been working at the 'Y'." She filled two glasses with water and returned to the den.

"So, Mr. Happy isn't very happy?" he asked, pulling food from the bag.

"Very funny," she returned, but she twisted her mouth to keep from smiling.

"So what do you want?"

"Everything," Lilly said. "But I'll start with chicken soup and maybe half a sub."

"When is the last time you ate?"

We Need A Little Christmas

"I don't know. Crackers at the 'Y'." She took a bite of the sub and moaned. "This is so good."

She felt his gaze on her, but was shameless. Smelly fish or not, Justin had come through with food.

He took a sip of water. "You've been avoiding me."

She nearly choked on a bite of sub. She could deny it, but was too tired for it. "I have been."

"I thought we were going to be friends," he said.

She shrugged. "I'm still bothered that you didn't tell me your real name."

"What's it going to take to fix that?"

"I don't know. This isn't the first time a man deceived me. The last time, he had a wife and children. It was awful." She stopped eating because her throat felt as if it closed.

He leaned toward her. "I don't have a wife or children. I don't even have a cat."

Her chest and throat still felt tight. She closed her eyes. "But you still lied," she whispered. "And I felt like such an idiot."

Silence stretched between them.

"I can understand that," he said.

"Can you?" she asked. "If I had lied to you, would you even be speaking to me?"

She watched his jaw tighten. "Fair. I want to fix it."

"I'm not sure you can," she said, her appetite gone.

"Well, I sure can't if you don't let me try."

Lilly sighed. "You're this rich bachelor. I'm just Lilly Johansen. Why would you want me?"

He leaned toward her and stared into her eyes. "Other than the fact that you're pretty amazing, I just do." Rising from the couch, he headed for the door. "Answer my call or text next time. I can't make it better if you won't let me."

Justin left and she stared at the remainder of her sub. Mr. Happy jumped up beside her and looked at her hopefully. She gave him a couple pieces of turkey then bundled up the sandwich and soup and put them in the refrigerator. Stinky fish, she tried to tell herself, but she wasn't sure if it was working.

Lilly exchanged a few text messages the next day with Justin, but the upcoming winter coat event kept her too busy to focus on him. Thank goodness. Saturday morning arrived and she joined several volunteers at the "Y". By the time they opened for the event, she was told that a line was forming around the block.

Lilly feared they would run out of coats. She was so grateful for the volunteers. Mid-morning, she caught sight of a familiar figure out of the side of her eye. She nearly got whiplash from taking a second glance at the volunteer who was indeed Justin.

We Need A Little Christmas

She gaped at him and a middle-aged woman volunteer nudged her. "He's hot, isn't he?"

Lilly snapped her mouth shut and glared at the woman. Shaking her head at herself, she shrugged. "He's all right if you like that type."

The woman chuckled. "Honey, I think he's every woman's type."

That comment didn't help Lilly's insecurities when it came to Justin, but she shook off her confusing feelings and focused on the next family asking for coats. Someone pressed a bottle of water in her hand, but the hours flew. At five pm, the coats were gone and Lilly resolved to try to collect more before Christmas. She made sure to thank everyone twice.

Justin stood in front of her. "Hungry?"

He knew her weakness. "I'm surprised you're still here."

"I may not be perfect, but I've got stamina," he told her.

The expression in his eyes was seductive and she felt that strange tumbling sensation in her belly, which she hoped was just hunger. For food.

"Well?" he asked. "There's a restaurant a few blocks over I think you would like. I can drive then take you back to your car after we eat."

"That's an offer I can't refuse," she said. "I'm starved and tired."

"But successful," he added and led her out of the building to his Jeep. He opened the door and helped her into the passenger seat.

Lilly groaned as she sank into the leather seat. "This feels so good. I don't know if I will be able to move for an hour."

"Maybe for food," Justin suggested with a sly grin and pulled away from his parking spot.

She closed her eyes and smiled. "Maybe. It was very nice of you to volunteer today. That was a surprise as were the coats."

"I sent the coats over a week ago."

She nodded then opened her eyes to look at him. "You really do like to keep your charity dealings on the down-low. No one knew who you were today. When the press showed up, you temporarily disappeared."

"I prefer to stay in the background. Before, I just preferred to write the checks and not get involved. I got more involved due to your terrible influence."

"Terrible?" she echoed. "That sounds like a change for the better."

"I'm not one of those business owners with a lot of extra time on their hands. I'm a working CEO. I have a responsibility to my employees and my customers," he said. "And I can't write checks for charity if I'm not taking care of my business."

We Need A Little Christmas

"Never thought of it that way, but I suppose you're right." She paused. "You still seemed a little anti-Christmas when I met you."

"And now?" he asked.

She thought about how he'd helped with the Tolinskis and helped decorate his brother's Christmas tree. "You've shown improvement."

"Good to know," he said in a dry tone and pulled alongside the curb of a trendy-looking diner. "Faint praise, but I'll take it." He got out of the car and ushered her into the diner which was already busy for the evening. "Two for dinner in a booth if you can find one."

The hostess looked at her seating chart and started to shake her head then glanced up at the tables. "Oh, one is opening up right now. Just give us a chance to clear the table and clean it."

Less than five minutes passed and they were led to a booth by the window. The hostess gave each of them menus and Lilly immediately opened hers. She began to read the choices and her mouth drooled. "Oh my gosh. How do I choose? Meatloaf, open-faced turkey sandwich with stuffing and mashed potatoes and chicken parmesan. I love chicken parmesan. I love Italian food. How do I choose?"

"You could choose one of each," he said.

She glanced at him to see if he was joking. "I can't eat that much."

"Take home," he said.

She shook her head. "I need to make a decision. I think I've got to go with the open-faced turkey sandwich. That's an all-around winner. What are you looking at? Tell me it's not the 'lite menu', or I'll feel bad."

"Well, I was looking at the grilled chicken salad with dressing on the side," he said.

"Oh, for Pete's sake—"

He laughed. "Just kidding. I'm getting the meatloaf and a beer."

"I'll take a chocolate milkshake with mine. Hey, carpe diem. I may be eating chicken nuggets from my freezer tomorrow night."

He met her gaze. "I like the way you enjoy food. You're not shy or prissy about it."

It was a genuine compliment, and it made her feel warm inside. "I'm not big on cooking, so I get excited about food I didn't get out of my freezer."

The server arrived at the table and took their orders.

"Are you happy with how the event went?" Justin asked.

She looked into his eyes and tried to tamp down her attraction to him, but he had become the most handsome man alive to her. His dark eyes and dark sense of humor, his strength, all got under her skin. Lilly told herself he had been untruthful and she sighed.

"I think it went pretty well. I did an informal event with the "Y" last year. Less coats, less people who needed them. In comparison, this was huge. One of the keys is finding people in need. Both last year and this year, I went downtown to areas where more homeless people seem to wander, and I tied some coats to lampposts encouraging people to take coats if they needed them.

"I didn't know you'd done that. It could be dangerous," he said.

"Life is dangerous, isn't it?"

He gave a slow nod. "Yeah, but you don't need to push things. Next time you decide to do something like that, give me a call."

The waitress delivered their meal and Lilly devoured hers. "Best open-faced turkey sandwich ever," she said, working on her mashed potatoes and stuffing.

"Said someone who's been on her feet all day. You could get excited about cardboard," he gently teased her.

"I've had cardboard pizza. Haven't you?"

A woman appeared beside their table. "Justin, I'm out with some friends and I saw you through the window. I hope I'm not interrupting. I just hadn't heard from you since we had drinks a few weeks ago."

Lilly took in the sight of the beautiful brunette and her bite of stuffing stuck in her throat. The woman's hair was perfectly curled, her make-up enhanced her ivory complexion and her outfit skimmed over her slim curves in invitation. Lilly was all too aware of the fact that whatever cosmetics she'd smeared on this morning had melted off and her hair was a unique blend of limp frizz beneath her wool cap.

"Hello there," she said to Lilly. "I'm Ava Gallimore. I've known Justin for over a year now. I'm sorry to interrupt your meal."

"No trouble," Lilly said. "Nice to meet you."

"Well, I won't keep you, but I wanted to tell you, Justin, that I've spotted a nice little property you may want to purchase and flip. I'll call you later about it. G'night now."

Justin shot Lilly a rueful look. "Forgive me for not introducing you, but I was swallowing my meatloaf. I couldn't get a word in edgewise."

Lilly nodded. "Same thing with a bite of my stuffing." She took a long draw from her milkshake. "Just curious. Do you know any normal-looking women? Are they all stunningly beautiful?"

Chapter 10

"There's cosmetic beauty and there's real beauty," Justin had answered her.

"Hmm. Sounds like you're hedging," she'd returned.

"I've never worked this hard to regain a woman's trust."

That said it all. Even after she arrived home from their dinner, her heart still felt as if it stopped as she remembered his words. At the same time, she wondered if she was beautiful enough, sophisticated enough, or just enough. He was a handsome, dynamic man. How could she hold his interest?

Lilly realized she was doubting herself as much or more than she was doubting him. Lilly frowned at the thought. She'd liked to believe that she'd risen above the loss of her mother, father and foster mother, that she had moved past the bad times and created a good life.

Taking a shower didn't wash away her questions about herself or Justin. The more she learned about him, the more she wanted to know. The more time she spent with him, the more time she wanted to be with him. Too physically tired for all her emotional meanderings, she collapsed in bed and fell asleep.

The next morning, Mr. Happy pawed at her face to awaken her. "It's too early," she said and glanced at the clock. Nine thirty am. "Oh, maybe not so early. You've been quite patient, haven't you?"

Mr. Happy meowed in response. Lilly petted her cat and took him to the kitchen. She filled his bowl with food and gave him fresh water. She seriously considered eating some of her leftovers from last night, but decided on cereal. The Tolinskis had hinted that they could use some help putting up a few more decorations, so she decided to visit the couple after she made herself a bit more presentable.

Two hours later, she had placed a wreath outside the Tolinskis bathroom door and helped set up a nativity scene. "Oh, it's perfect," Mrs. Tolinski said. "I can't thank you enough."

"It's too much clutter," Mr. Tolinski grumbled. "More for me to run into with my walker or chair. We already have a tree inside and a wreath on the front door. That's more than enough."

"Oh, quit being such a Scrooge. Admit it. These decorations cheer you up," Mrs. Tolinski told him.

"Well, the lights are nice, I guess. Thank you for putting up with my wife's demands," he said to Lilly.

We Need A Little Christmas

"I'm happy to help," Lilly said and dropped a kiss on the older man's cheek. Her cell phone rang, distracting her. "Excuse me. Hello, this is Lilly."

"Lilly, this is Francine Thomas. I'm afraid I have bad news. Justin has been in an automobile accident. He's at Springfield Memorial Hospital in the emergency room. I'm his emergency contact, but they didn't tell me his condition. I'm going to the hospital now. I thought you might want to know."

Lilly's heart sank to her feet. Her blood ran cold through her veins. She responded automatically. "Thank you so much for letting me know. I'll be there as soon as possible." She turned to the Tolinskis. "There's been an emergency. I have to go."

"Oh, dear," Mrs. Tolinski said. "You've gone pale. Are you sure you're able to drive? What has happened?"

"It's Justin," she said. "He has been in an accident."

"Justin?" Mrs. Tolinski echoed. "I thought your friend was Dane."

"They're the same. Please say a prayer," Lilly said and ran out the door, her eyes filling with tears. Jerking her Volkswagon out of its space, she raced toward the hospital.

Her mind and heart full of worry and regret, she prayed and cried at the same time. "Please don't let him die. He's a good one. He seems cranky, but he's really good," she said to God. She sobbed. "Oh, God. I want him to live just so I can know him better."

She pulled into the hospital parking lot. Unfortunately, this wasn't the hospital where her neighbor Roberta worked. She dashed inside to the emergency room desk. "I'm here for Justin Burgess."

"He's being treated," the attendant told her. "Are you a relative?"

Lilly's heart sank. She considered telling a lie. The same way Justin had told her a lie. She bit her lip. "No."

"I'm sorry. I can't give you any more information at this time."

Not knowing what to do with herself, Lilly walked toward the waiting room. Perhaps she should call Francine Thomas. At the same time, she didn't want to interrupt the woman if she was by Justin's side. She sank into a chair and stared out the window.

What if she had waited too late to forgive Justin?

Closing her eyes, she shook her head, vowing to make a fresh start with him if she got the chance.

An hour passed, but it felt like ten. A woman approached her, waving her hand in front of Lilly's face. "Lilly," the white-haired woman said. "It's Francine. Francine Thomas. Are you okay?"

We Need A Little Christmas

Lilly nodded. "Sorry. I'm in a daze. How is Justin?"

"He was on his way to one of his stores to cover for a general manager who was ill. A truck hit the driver's side. He was bleeding quite a bit, so they took him into surgery right away and removed his spleen. He also has a broken rib," Francine said, sitting next to her.

"Oh, no," Lilly said. "Will he be okay?"

"The doctors think so. I'll make sure you can see him as soon as he gets out of recovery. His beloved Jeep is a goner," Francine said.

"I think I want him to get a tank," Lilly said.

Francine rubbed Lilly's arm and smiled. "I had a good feeling about you from the beginning, dear."

Hours passed, and Justin was finally wheeled out of recovery to a hospital room. Lilly went in as soon as she was allowed. "Hi," she said in a soft voice. "Just rest and get better."

Justin's eyes fluttered open. "Am I in heaven?"

Lilly didn't know whether to laugh or cry. "When your medication wears off, you won't be asking that question. I've been terribly worried about you."

"Want me to stick around even though I'm not perfect?" he asked.

"You're as perfect as I'll ever want," she told him, but he had already drifted off to sleep.

Justin awakened, feeling as if his body ached from head to toe. A vague memory of the accident slid through his anesthesia-filled brain. His gut hurt and he could hardly breathe. He groaned.

Lilly immediately appeared beside him, her hair tousled and her eyes bleary from sleep. "Are you hurting? I'll ask the nurse for some pain medication."

He wondered if he was seeing an apparition. "Are you really here? Lilly?"

She swiped at her eyes. "Of course I'm here. Where else would I be?"

"You know I'm in love with you," he told her. "You know I want you to marry me."

Her eyes rounded. "Oh." She seemed to try to catch her breath. "I think this might be the anesthesia talking."

"It's not," he said. "But I could use some more pain meds. I feel like a truck hit me."

"That's because it did," Lilly said and called the nurse.

Epilogue

Five days later after Justin had returned home and Lilly had returned to working half-days, she called to tell him she was coming to his condominium after work, as usual. Justin had given her a key and the valet now knew her by name.

Against his doctor's advice, he'd taken his first trip out this morning by himself and he was paying for it. His chest hurt enough to make him say a few words under his breath that didn't include Merry Christmas.

He'd ordered Italian and lit the gas fireplace. He considered popping a pain pill, but he didn't want to be accused of being under the influence. Leaning back in his chair, he tried to rest.

It seemed that barely a moment passed and he heard Lilly's voice. "Thank you very much," she said to someone at his door. "It smells delicious."

He blinked, wondering how long he had been asleep. "Hi there, beautiful," he called.

She came into the room wearing a smile. "I was hoping you would keep resting. You were snoring when I first arrived."

How romantic, he thought. "I have something I need to discuss with you."

"Okay," she said. "Do you want to eat first?"

"Not really," he said.

Her face fell. "Oh."

"This won't take long," he said. "I can't kneel at the moment. I'll do it later if you want. But I'm not at all medicated and I'm hurting like the devil." He reached for the jeweler's box on the table beside him and stood.

"Oh, no, you should be sitting," she said, rushing toward him.

"Lilly Johansen, I love you. Will you marry me?" he asked and flipped open the box.

Lilly gaped at him then the diamond ring. "Omigoodness. I didn't need a ring. And this diamond is just way too big."

Justin couldn't help chuckling. How many women would complain that their engagement diamond was too large? "I can't go out again for awhile, so I guess you'll just have to make do with this one." He looked into the gaze of the woman he loved more than life. "Will you marry me?"

"Oh, yes," Lilly said and pressed her mouth against his. "I love you, love you, love you. Can we still check in on the Tolinskis and Roberta?"

"Yes, of course we can."

"Merry Christmas, my forever love," she said to him.

Justin pulled her against him. He knew this would be the first of many wonderful Christmases because of Lilly.

Made in the USA
Middletown, DE
08 January 2025